Originally published as *Zaza speelt doktertje* in Belgium and the Netherlands by Clavis Uitgeverij, 2009
English translation from the Dutch by Clavis Publishing Inc., New York

Visit us on the Web at www.clavisbooks.com.

Calling Dr. Zaza written and illustrated by Mylo Freeman

ISBN 978-1-60537-375-1

This book was printed in February 2020 at Wai Man Book Binding (China) Ltd. Flat A, 9/F., Phase 1,
Kwun Tong Industrial Centre, 472-484 Kwun Tong Road, Kwun Tong, Kowloon, H.K.

First Edition
10 9 8 7 6 5 4 3

MYLO FREEMAN

Calling Dr. Zaza

Clavis
NEW YORK

Zaza wants to play, but her animal friends
don't feel well. Calling Dr. Zaza!

Does Rosie have an earache?
Zaza takes a look in Rosie's ear.
Rosie will feel better soon.

Time to listen to Bobby's heart.

Boom-boom. Boom-boom. Boom-boom.

What a beautiful sound!

Bobby's heart sounds perfect.

George Giraffe has a sore throat.

"Say *aah*!" says Zaza.

George opens his mouth and Zaza takes a good look.

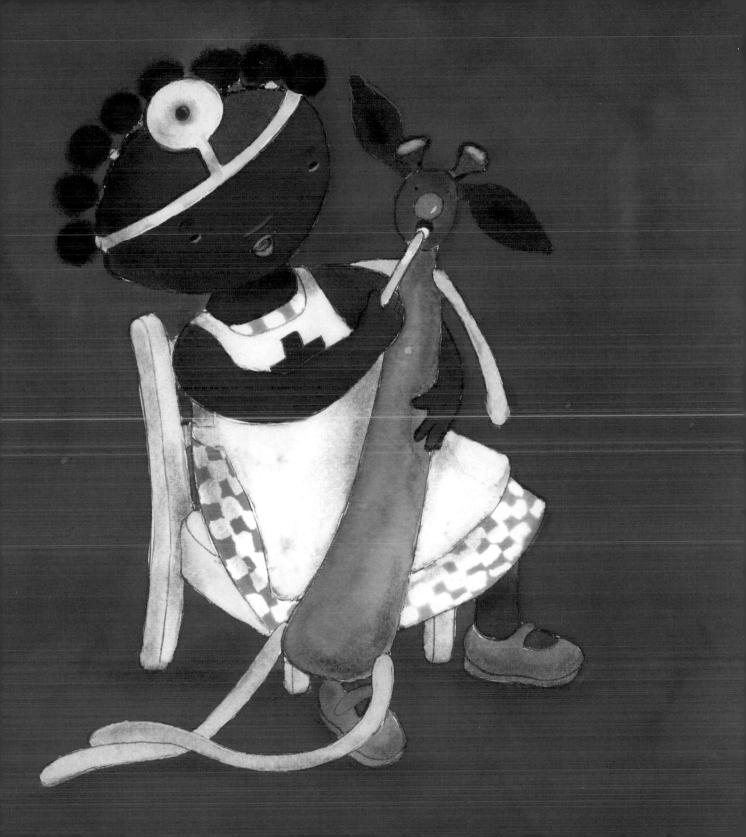

Pinkie feels a little warm.

Does she have a fever?

No. Her temperature is just right.

What about Mo?
Mo has a scratch on his head.
Zaza puts a bandage on it.
All better!

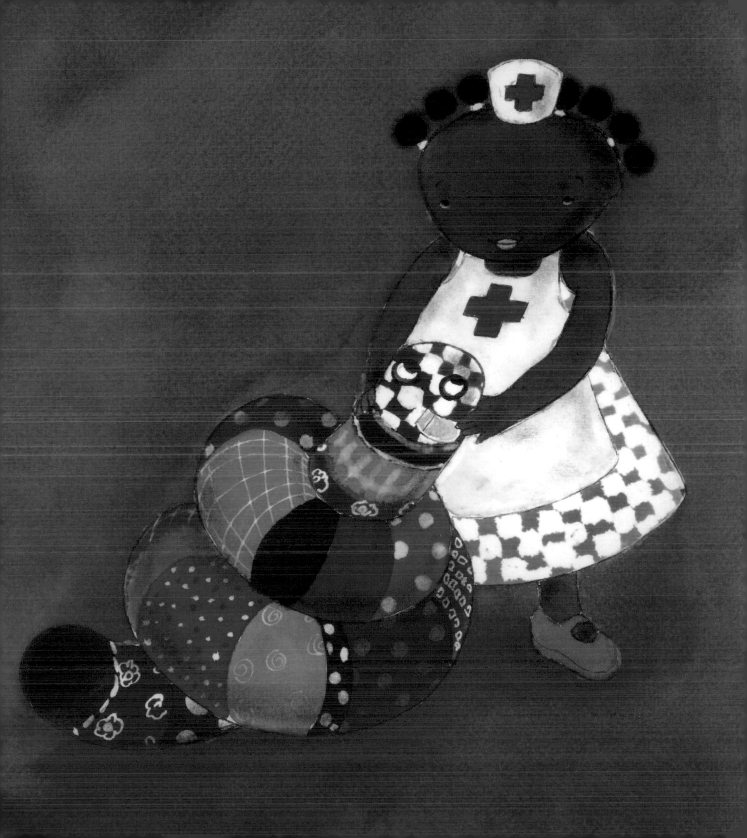

But guess what?
All the other animals want bandages too!

What a busy day.
All of Zaza's animal friends feel much better.
They just need one more thing—
a big kiss from Dr. Zaza.
Now everyone is ready to play!